A WORLD FULL OF
MONSTERS

To my wife, Dorothy, and our sons,
John Troy, Jr., Gregory Lamont, Garrick Desmond,
and Jackson Kinte
—J.T.M.

With love for Jonathon, Katherine, and Hayley—
all of whom are monsters only part of the time
—M.B.

A World Full of Monsters
Text copyright © 1986 by John Troy McQueen Illustrations copyright © 1986 by Marc Brown
Printed in the U.S.A. All rights reserved. www.harperchildrens.com
Library of Congress Cataloging-in-Publication Data
McQueen, John Troy.
  A world full of monsters / by John Troy McQueen ; illustrations by Marc Brown.
                              p.   cm.
  Summary: A little boy explains away the noises of the night by telling himself a story about a world full of friendly
monsters.
  ISBN 0-06-029769-7 — ISBN 0-06-029770-0 (lib. bdg.)
  [1. Monsters—Fiction. 2. Fear—Fiction. 3. Night—Fiction.] I. Brown, Marc Tolon, ill. II. Title.
PZ7.M478825Wo. 2001   [E]   85-48257
         1 2 3 4 5 6 7 8 9 10   ❖   First HarperCollins Edition, 2001

A WORLD FULL OF
MONSTERS

JOHN TROY McQUEEN

ILLUSTRATED BY
MARC BROWN

HARPERCOLLINSPUBLISHERS

A long time ago,

when my grandparents' grandparents
were growing up,
monsters were everywhere.

There weren't any electric lights.

There weren't any cars.

There weren't many big machines.

But there were monsters.

There were monsters in the city.

There were monsters in the country.

In the city monsters were policemen.

The mayor was a monster.

Monsters carried garbage to the city dump.

Monsters put out fires.

Monsters were everywhere you looked.
When you saw one, you just said,
"Hi, Monster," and kept on walking.

In the country, monsters ran the farms.
Monsters cut the hay…

monsters milked the cows…

monsters fed the pigs...

monsters fed the chickens.

Monsters were everywhere you looked.

Monsters played football.

Monsters went bowling.

Monsters played baseball.

Monsters even played tennis.

Monsters were everywhere.

There aren't many monsters left nowadays....

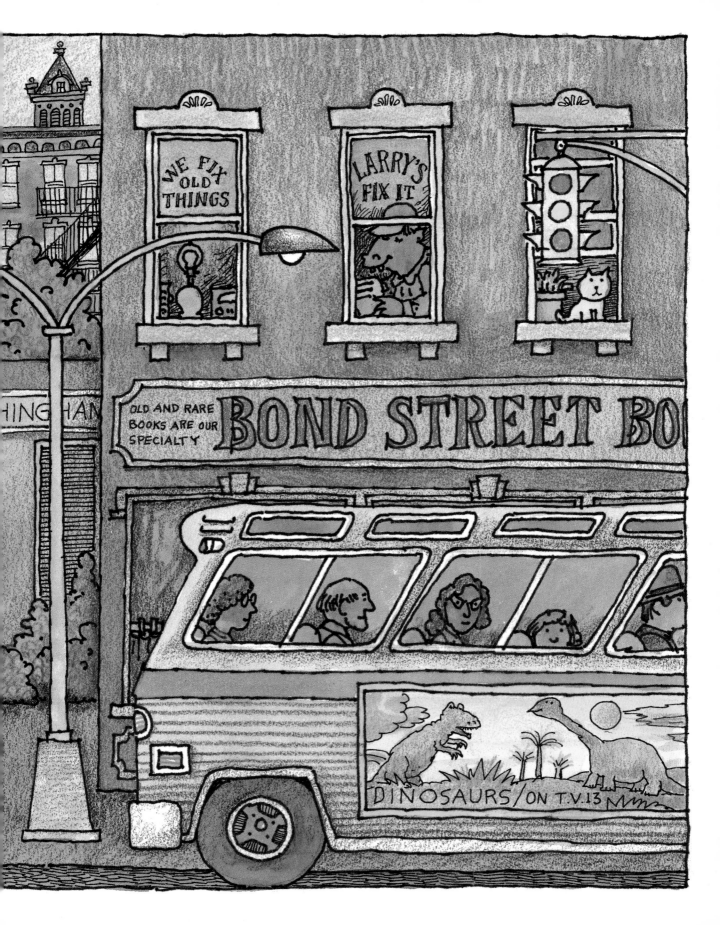

But at night when I hear the screech, screech, screech sound…

the tick, tick, tick sound...

the scratch, scratch, scratch sound...

the squeak, squeak, squeak sound...

or the drip, drip, drip sound,
I know that it's the sound
of monsters.

When one comes into my room,
I'll just say, "Hi, Monster!"

and go back to sleep.